IN THE NIGHT KITCHEN

MAURICE SENDAK

HARPER & ROW, PUBLISHERS

FOR SADIE AND PHILIP

WHERE THE BAKERS WHO BAKE TILL THE DAWN SO WE CAN HAVE CAKE IN THE MORN MIXED MICKEY IN BATTER, CHANTING:

AND THEY PUT THAT BATTER UP TO BAKE

A DELICIOUS MICKEY-CAKE.

SO HE SKIPPED FROM THE OVEN & INTO BREAD DOUGH
ALL READY TO RISE IN THE NIGHT KITCHEN.

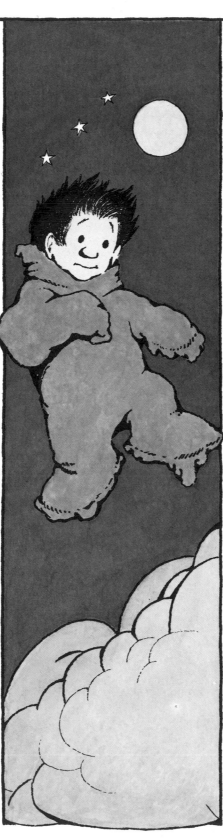

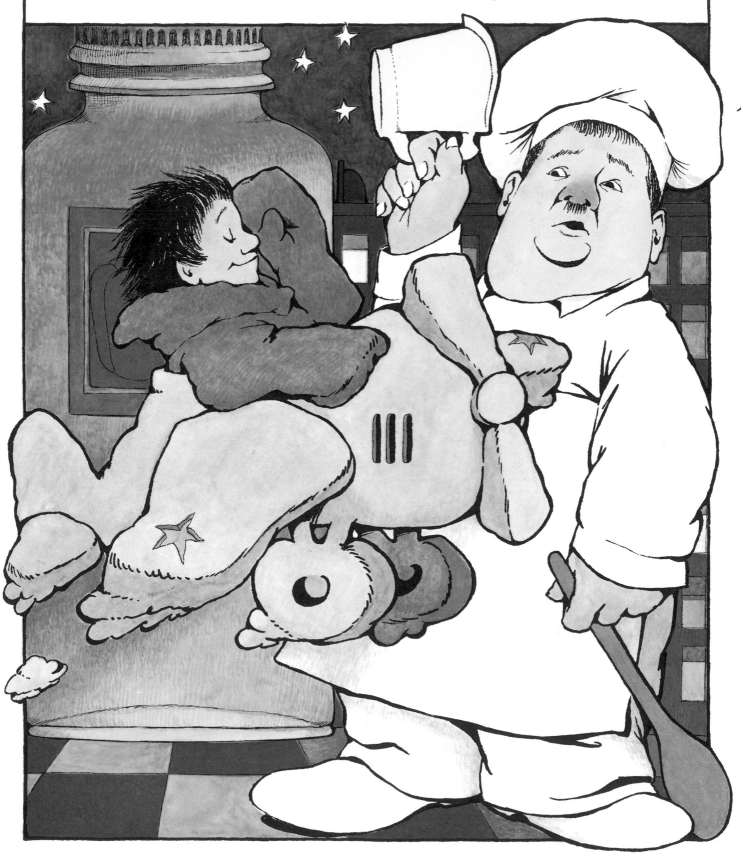

WHEN THE BAKERS RAN UP
WITH A MEASURING CUP, HOWLING:

THEN HE SWAM TO THE TOP, POURING MILK
FROM HIS CUP INTO BATTER BELOW—

SO THE BAKERS THEY MIXED IT
AND BEAT IT AND BAKED IT.

COCK·a·DOODLE DOO!

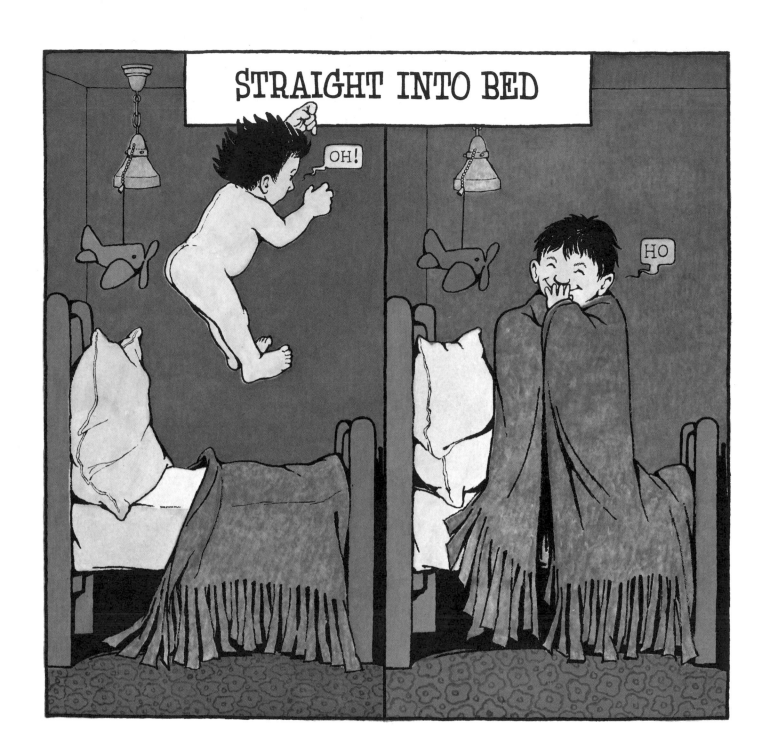